God's Messenger

By

Caroline DuBois Hutton

ISBN: 0 - 9742894 - 0 - X

Published by
Huttonelectronicpublishing.com
160 Compo Road N., Westport, CT 06880-2102

To God's messengers, whomever, whatever and
wherever they may be.

'Be not forgetful to entertain strangers: for thereby
some have entertained angels unawares'.
Hebrews 13.8

'God has made his darkness
Beautiful with thee'.
Alfred, Lord Tennyson, *In Memoriam*

Night fell gently on the city. It was late May and the air was softly scented with the perfume of spring blossoms. Across the square, heavy in its profusion of horse chestnuts, one light shone through the upper windows of a tall and narrow house.

The windows were unlighted in the dusk, save for the weak beacon that burned from the top floor. The occupants of the house did not notice the coming of the dark, for in an upstairs bedroom a child lay dying.

He lay in a single bed whose sheets and blankets were rumpled and twisted. Mother straightened the bedclothes, then sat on the bed, while the sister knelt at his side. Both were dark of hair and pale of skin. The mother's hair was a short cap, while the sister's long tresses spilled down her back in a luxurious waterfall.

It was most certainly a boy's room, filled with posters of racing bikes and *Star Wars* and rock stars. In the corner was a bench with a set of weights, while under a window stood a drafting table holding a half assembled model car. Battery operated, it would never be finished or run – on a fine afternoon under the horse chestnut trees in the square.

An easel in a corner held a half-finished painting of a humming bird poised at the center of a hollyhock, its shimmering feathers picked out, lovingly, painstakingly, by a brush with a single hair. It, too, would never be finished.

The boy's bright, golden hair was the only radiance in the darkened room. It seemed to have drawn all the strength from the once robust body, now wasted and consumed by illness.

The mother held her son as if he were still the baby of many years ago; his sister clasped his hand. It was the hand she had clung to as a small child whenever she was frightened or especially happy. The brother had rarely let her down. His hand had led her gently but firmly through many of life's pleasures and trials, but it would lead her no more.

The clock in the downstairs hall struck the quarter hour and the child grew restless as he prepared for a journey which would leave behind the two he loved the best. It was a journey only he could make and he must make it alone. He had spent but sixteen years on earth, but now he was summoned home.

He looked up at his mother and gave one small sigh. The hand that lay in his sister's grew slack. Slowly and imperceptibly his body released the spirit that had been his pilot through life.

His soul left his earthly body and began its journey back to God.

The spirit had been restless, longing for all that life could not give and now it sought peace, though there was still a thread holding him to life and he felt fear of the unknown.

The separation of body and soul were so recent that the earthly concerns of the child who had just died were with him still. Had he died later in life, wherein his earthly affairs were settled, his passage would have taken but an instant.

But the child was only sixteen when he died and he left this life possessing a knowledge of things left undone on earth. In that timeless moment between the here and the there the boy's spirit had shackles to shed before he could truly leave the concerns of his life and stand in the presence of God. Of the father who had abandoned him, he had no concern. It was his mother and sister, who, even now, in that dark and lonely room, mourned his death, that kept his ties to life as he had known it on earth from severing.

All the cares of human life must be shed and the soul arrive weightless and entirely separate from all things earthly before it can stand in the presence of its Maker.

As the child's soul began its ascent toward God, it recognized a huge clamor below: the noise made by all humankind. The din quickly gave way to the mists enveloping the earth which were rising, carrying him up and ever upward.

The clamor receded, becoming lower and farther in the distance. The mists swirled in, darker and darker, carrying with them a bitter cold, which enveloped the soul of the boy and bore him onward.

WAS THIS ALL THERE WAS?

THE ESSENCE OF NOTHING?

Darkness fell and became perfect: the absence of light.

Ahead lay the mouth of a valley, long and twisting and shrouded in the deepest gloom.

From the black abyss a presence appeared, familiar Though undefined. It was a glimmer in the mist, coming closer and closer, warming the boy's soul and giving him strength to continue his journey.

Brighter and brighter the presence glowed, until it shone with such a brilliant light that would have blinded anyone with earthly vision, for the creature had recently been in the presence of God, whose perfect glory it reflected.

Soul and presence drew nigh one to the other, and the soul recognized a celestial dog, though a dog never seen on earth. Its coat shone like the sun and moon and all the stars, a fiery, glittering brightness that was beyond human comprehension. Its eyes burned amber through the dark with a light never experienced by the boy during his life.

As the boy would have done on earth, he reached out to pat the dog and his hand closed over that most familiar feeling object: a cold, wet nose.

In that instant the transfer from the corporal to the spiritual took place and any lingering earthly bonds broke and the soul took flight. The gossamer cord that had bound the boy to life and to the life of his mother and sister parted with total finality and his soul entered the Valley of the Shadow.

As the child's soul traversed the Valley, the blackness faded to gray then to shadowy mists full of promise and color...mauve, moss, midnight blue. At the end of the Valley shone a shaft of sunlight, luminous and beckoning.

The mists on the hillside dispersed as the sky grew milky with the approach of morning, the eternal morning of the soul. Light played over the hillside bordering the Valley, which became lush and verdant. The child's soul approached the light with joy and expectation and was transported through its shining beams.

From a great distance came the sound of music, such as had never been heard on earth. The soul felt a presence, tender and compassionate, and it became totally at peace. There was a tiny beacon of perfect joy as the soul entered the lucidity of the greater light, which grew ever brighter and the music swelled until it seemed all the galaxies of infinity were singing. Almost close enough to touch rose the morning star that heralds the break of dawn.

The heavenly dog began his descent that would ultimately take him to the home in the city the boy had left behind.

Lower and lower he sank, through the coldness of the mists, down through the loneliness. In his passage he lost the brightness that once had been his, and his beautiful body shrank and contracted and began to resemble that of the lowliest cur. His fur turned to dingy black, interspersed in dusty tan on his underside and his muzzle. The noble brow disappeared into a snout with the pointiest of noses and a high widow's peak, the black surrounding the dusty tan. The eyes changed from fiery amber to the most ordinary of browns. Yet just on the tip of his tail, five hairs remained of the purest gold, a reminder of whence the dog had come.

His body gained weight and substance as he descended and he lost the knowledge of that bright place from where he once had come.

The clamor of earth came to him, a deafening din in his ears.

At last his feet struck the cold and damp of a city pavement. The long night was nearly spent. With no hesitation he trotted down the long, empty street and turned a corner. He knew where he was going.

The dog turned another corner and stopped across the street from a tall and narrow house. He leaned up against the railing of a square that was overhung with the weight of horse chestnut blossoms bursting from the boughs. He sat down and scratched. His feet hurt from the long trip across the city.

The sun rose over the rooftops, signaling a perfect day. The dog continued to sit and wait patiently. He had not long to wait.

In the house a shade went up, then another, first in an upstairs room, then in the big window on the ground floor which faced the street. A woman opened the door and came out onto the top step. Her face was drawn and sad and her shoulders drooped as she stood looking out at the beginnings of the perfect morning.

The dog shambled across the street and up the steps, where he cringed in front of the woman. His coat was a mess, patchy and dull, and his ribs stood out sharply against his black and tan coat. Hesitatingly, he thumped his tail once against the balustrade.

The woman started and looked deeply into his eyes and a kind of recognition appeared on her face. The corners of her mouth turned up almost imperceptibly and she held wide the door as she reached out her hand to the dog.

As he crossed the threshold, the dog paused to put his muzzle trustingly into the woman's outstretched hand. His nose was wet and cold against her palm. He entered the hall and flopped, gratefully, onto the rug.

The woman bent to pat him, them vanished down the stairs, returning a moment later with a bowl of water. She placed it beside the dog and he lifted his head and drank thirstily, slopping some of the water onto the rug. He lay a moment longer, as if gathering his strength, then lifted his nose and sniffed the air. He raised himself up, gave a little shake, and ambled up the stairs to the second floor. He trod silently on the carpeted stairs as he ascended.

The woman followed him. At the first landing the dog paused and sniffed again, then continued on his way up to the top of the house. The daughter emerged from her room and followed the mother and the dog upstairs. On the uppermost landing the dog paused yet again. His pointed snout rose upward and he sniffed once again, quickly. He put the nose around the door to the room where last night the child had died, and pushed it wide so all three could enter.

Mother and daughter crowded in the doorway they had left in such misery only the night before.

The dog did not hesitate for a second. He climbed easily onto the rumpled bed, resting one paw on the flattened pillow. He scratched at the bedclothes, seeking to make a more comfortable nest for himself, then turned around precisely three times. He settled down with a sigh and what looked like a satisfied expression on his scruffy face. He had come a long way and he was very tired. With another sigh he shut his eyes and fell asleep.

The daughter looked in amazement at her mother.

"Where did he come from?" she asked.

Mother did not hesitate for a second.

"Your brother sent him," she said, and her arm crept around her daughter's shoulders.

Together they watched the dog, so peacefully asleep in the bed so lately vacated by its rightful owner.

At that instant the child's soul entered the loving arms of The Father, there to dwell in peace and joy for all eternity. He was at one with the light and the music and enfolded into the glory of Almighty God and his journey was done.

Who can know in heavenly time how long as the passage of the boy's soul upward and of the dog's, downward? In celestial time it was less than the blink of a human eye, whose measure is not taken in heaven.

It is only certain that both the soul of the child and the Messenger had arrived safely, each to his appointed home.

On a quiet hillside in New England there is a village of stone…monuments to those loved ones who have gone before. Among them is a child's headstone. It has the dates for his birth and death and a paraphrase from *Peter Pan*, apt perhaps for a boy who never grew to manhood. In the dappled shade of a maple tree, the stone reads

'Death Must Be The Greatest Adventure Of Them All'.

Amen